Written by Tim Collins
Illustrations by John Bigwood
Cover design by John Bigwood
Edited by Jonny Marx

First published in Great Britain in 2017 by Buster Books,
an imprint of Michael O'Mara Books Limited,
9 Lion Yard, Tremadoc Road, London SW4 7NQ

 www.busterbooks.co.uk

 Buster Children's Books

 @BusterBooks

A CIP catalogue record for this book is available from the British Library.

ISBN: 978-1-78055-480-8

10 9 8 7 6 5 4 3 2 1

Printed and bound in April 2017 by CPI Group (UK) Ltd, 108 Beddington Lane,
Croydon, CR0 4YY, United Kingdom.

Papers used by Michael O'Mara Books are natural, recyclable products
made from wood grown in sustainable forests. The manufacturing processes
conform to the environmental regulations of the country of origin.

COSMIC COLIN

Hairy
Hamster Horror

BUSTER

4

CHAPTER ONE

That's how the holidays had gone so far, with Nuclear Dragon Slayer Henderson twitching his nose and me staring.

Nuclear Dragon Slayer Henderson is our school hamster. He was named by a boy from my class called Jake Henderson.

I'd agreed to look after him for the holidays. I thought I'd be able to teach him some amazing tricks.

Or at the very least, get him to run on his wheel. But all he did was stare at me and twitch his little pink nose.

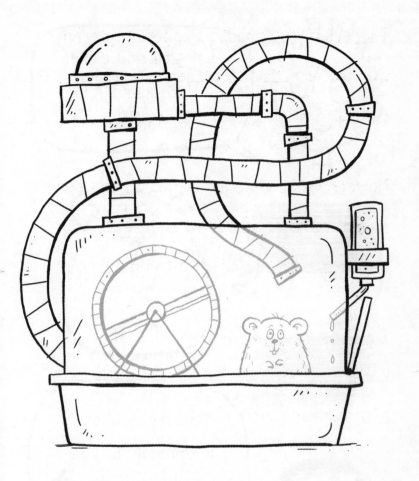

I was still waiting for him to do something
when Harry called round.

I'm glad you came. This hamster is so boring.

Squeak.

So that's what a hamster is. I've only seen the giant ones in the Andromeda Galaxy.

A planet with giant hamsters? Sounds weird.

They might say the same about a planet with tiny, bald-bodied humans!

Don't be rude about Earth!

I've got an idea! Why don't we go to the Andromeda Galaxy right now? If you want to see hamsters doing interesting stuff, it's the place to go.

My heart lifted at the idea of going off in the spacebin again. I love Harry's spacebin. It can take us ...

ANYWHERE IN TIME AND SPACE

I was about to agree, when I remembered about Nuclear Dragon Slayer Henderson. I'd promised to look after him, so I could hardly abandon him and go off on an adventure.

I can't go. Something might happen to Nuclear Dragon Slayer Henderson. One time, the school hamster died when a boy called Oliver Hughes was meant to be looking after it. He forgot to feed it and it died. He threw it away and bought a new one from a pet shop, but the markings were different so he got found out.

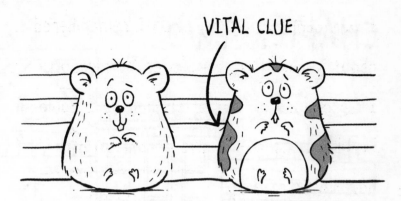

VITAL CLUE

You're forgetting that my spacebin is a time machine. However long we spend on the planet, I'll bring us back two minutes after we leave.

Okay. Let's go!

CHAPTER TWO

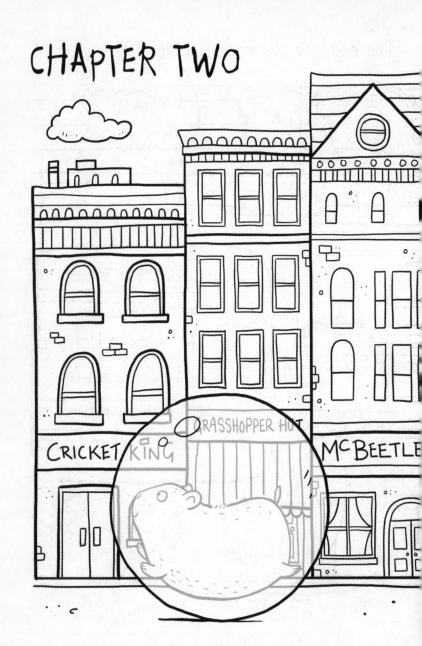

CRICKET KING   GRASSHOPPER HUT   MᶜBEETLE

The hamster planet was brilliant ... at first.

PET SHOP

The creatures were packed into fast-food restaurants, munching on beetles and crickets that were as big as cats and dogs.

They were speeding down the roads inside giant plastic balls.

And they were scurrying above us in tubes that jutted out of office blocks.

I was really enjoying the planet, until I remembered I'd left the door to Nuclear Dragon Slayer Henderson's cage open.

We need to go back! I haven't shut the hamster's cage!

It doesn't matter how long we spend here, remember? We'll still arrive back just after we left, so he's in no danger.

Oh, yeah. I forgot.

Anyway, we can't leave until we've seen the Great Wheel. No visit is complete without it.

I knew Harry was right, but I couldn't stop myself imagining that Nuclear Dragon Slayer Henderson was crawling out of his cage and getting lost or stuck somewhere.

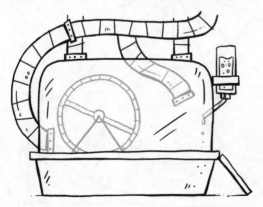

Time travel is VERY confusing.

The Great Wheel was an extraordinary
sight, just as Harry had said.

The **ENORMOUS** wheel contained
12 smaller ones, all powered by hamsters.

I was so distracted I forgot all about
Nuclear Dragon Slayer Henderson. I also
failed to notice the dark figure creeping
up behind me. By the time I felt a claw
closing around me, it was too late.

CHAPTER THREE

What's he saying?

Hang on ... I just need to reach the translation button on my space communicator.

Squeak, squeak, squeak!

Oh no! He says we'll be great to show to his class. I think he must be a teacher.

Squeak - squeak! Squeak!

It's even worse. He's saying he's going to take us to school right now in his car.

Why is that worse?

The hamster carried us to a car park and stopped in front of one of the giant plastic balls. They all looked the same to me, and I had no idea how he knew which one was his. Maybe they use smell instead of number plates.

He opened a door at the back of the ball
and threw us in. Then he stepped inside,
locked the hatch and got down on all fours.

He shifted his front paws and the ball
started to roll.

Harry jumped on the hamster's back and grabbed hold of his shirt. I clambered up after him.

The hamster steered the ball out of the car park and on to a main road.

He started to run faster.

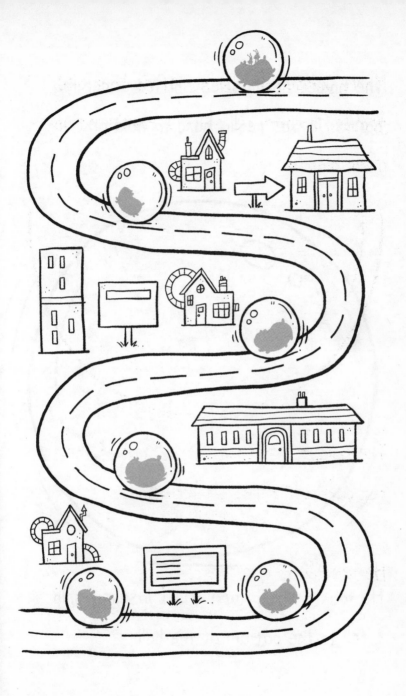

The hamster's muscles shifted under my hands. It was really hard to hold on.

He took a sharp turn and I lost my grip. I fell to the bottom of the ball.

Then the bottom became the top . . .

Then it was the bottom again.

The ball was going so fast I stayed stuck to the side, which at least meant I didn't get flung around.

But I was very, very dizzy.

Harry was shouting, but I couldn't hear what he was saying. Everything was becoming a blur and I felt sleepy.

CHAPTER FOUR

When I woke up, I was in my bed. All that stuff about giant hamsters and plastic balls had just been a bad dream. None of it had happened, and now I was safely back in my sawdust with my drinking bottle and my running wheel and ...

AARRRGGHH! It HAD all happened!

The teacher hamster really had taken us prisoner, and now I was trapped in a plastic cage. Through the clear walls, I could see rows of giant chairs facing a whiteboard.

Harry was curled up in the sawdust next to me, so I prodded him awake.

Quick! Summon the spacebin and get us out of this plastic prison.

I can't. We've gone too far away and it's out of range. But it doesn't matter. I heard the teacher squeaking to himself last night. He's going to take us out and show us to his pupils when they arrive. We can wriggle free and escape then. In the meantime, I recommend the bowl of dried worms in the corner. They're surprisingly tasty.

I slumped down on the sawdust and stared through the plastic. Eventually, the hamster teacher came in and tinkered with his laptop and projector. Soon after, the pupils filed in and took their seats.

They were just as badly behaved as most human pupils. One was pulling the whiskers of the hamster next to him.

Another was chewing her worksheet and
spitting it on to the girl in front.

Another was munching on a beetle.
The teacher told her
to stop, but she
kept chewing.

There was even a lazy hamster sitting at the back of the class with his paws folded and his feet up on the desk, staring out of the window.

There's a pupil like that in every class, even a hamster class.

When the lesson started, the teacher pointed to our cage and squeaked. The pupils instantly jumped up and crowded round us.

I could hear the teacher squealing behind them. If he was telling them to get back to their chairs, it wasn't working.

One of the pupils reached into our cage and lifted me on to the wheel. I began running, and the hamster giggled and clapped. My legs got really tired, so I stopped and flopped on to the sawdust beside the wheel.

The hamsters weren't happy. One of them lifted me right back on to the wheel, and wouldn't stop squeaking until I ran some more.

I kept going until sweat was pouring down my back and my tongue was hanging out. I couldn't believe I was exhausting myself just to impress a bunch of big hamsters. In the space of just one day, my life had really hit rock bottom.

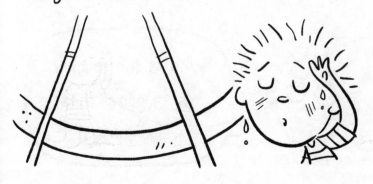

The teacher yelled even louder and they finally returned to their seats.

He clicked on his laptop and the image of a strange creature appeared on the whiteboard.

Why is the teacher talking about those weird things?

Err ... that's what he thinks we are.

What? We look NOTHING like them.

They're about the same size as us and they don't have any fur, so it's hard for them to tell the difference. I'm sure there are plenty of humans who can't tell the difference between a hamster, a gerbil, a chinchilla, a guinea pig and a mouse.

45

1. HAMSTER
2. GERBIL
3. CHINCHILLA
4. GUINEA PIG
5. MOUSE

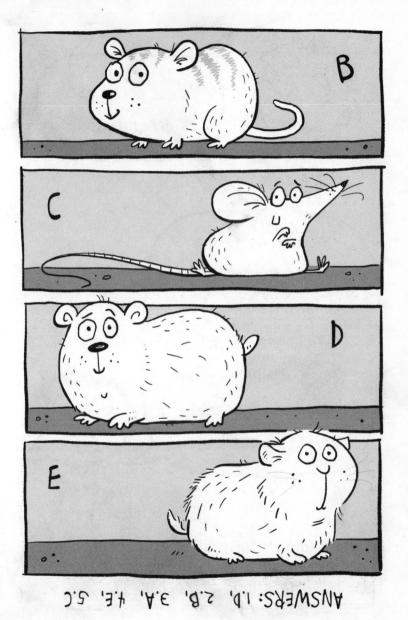

What are those creatures?

According to the teacher they're called 'doldrums'. They live underground, and they eat worms. That explains the food he put in our cage.

As the teacher continued squeaking, Harry's face fell into a look of horror.

What is it? What has he said?

He said that doldrums can be vicious, and the only way to calm them down is to burp in their faces. He said he's going to take us out and pass us round, and they should all burp on us!

OH NO!

CHAPTER FIVE

It was so horrible. The hamsters handed
us around and belched in our faces.
The horrible stench of beetles, crickets
and worms rose up from their stomachs
and filled my nostrils.

I felt sick, and forgot all about our escape plan.

I only remembered it when I spotted Harry. He'd wriggled free and was scampering across the floor. The hamsters were shrieking and pointing down at him.

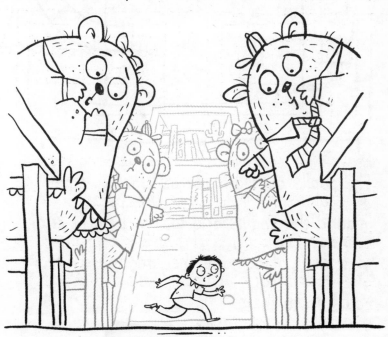

The teacher grabbed me and threw me back
into the cage. I leant against the plastic
and watched as he chased Harry around
the classroom.

The pupils darted aside as Harry weaved
around the chairs and tables. I don't know
what sort of damage they thought Harry
could do to them.

Harry scuttled under some drawers and the teacher had to sweep him out with a broom.

He grabbed Harry and tossed him back into the cage next to me.

I'm sorry I forgot our plan to escape. The burps made me feel ill.

Never mind. I'm sure we'll get another chance.

The teacher returned to his COMPLETELY INCORRECT lesson about us. He showed pictures of the doldrums lurking in dark underground lairs that looked nothing like cosy human houses.

Squeak, squeak, squeak!

Harry glanced at his space communicator.

This is great news! The teacher wants someone to take us home over the holidays, which start tonight. With just one hamster looking after us, we're bound to break free.

All the hamsters stuck their paws in the air to volunteer. All, except for the lazy one at the back, that is. He just kept looking out of the window.

The teacher strode over to him and squeaked.

What's going on?

Even better news. The teacher has decided that the lazy hamster should look after us, to teach him about responsibility. With that lazy rodent in charge, it'll be even easier to escape.

CHAPTER SIX

When school was over, the lazy hamster grabbed our cage and wandered back to his house.

He took us up to his room and plonked us in the corner. After that, he just slumped back on his sawdust, chewed on a dead cricket and ignored us.

We shouted and banged on the cage, but the lazy hamster didn't hear.

Oh no! He wasn't paying any attention in class. He's got no idea how to look after us. We'll starve!

No we won't. We've got our bowl of dried worms and our water tank. We can survive on those if we ration them.

And what about the spacebin? We just left it out on the street. One of those giant hamster balls could smash it, and then we'd be stuck here forever.

Oh ... I suppose you're right. In that case, let's go back to shouting and banging on the cage.

HEY! HEY! HEY!

The lazy hamster didn't even glance at us. He soon fell into a deep sleep and began to snore.

Harry broke off a piece of worm and handed it to me. It tasted of soil and leather, and I had to force myself to swallow it. I couldn't believe I'd have to survive on worms until we were free. If only doldrums ate pizza or chips instead.

As I munched my disgusting snack, I
tried to think of a way to escape. Then
I remembered the story I'd told Harry.
The one about the boy who'd accidentally
killed the school hamster and threw it away.

If we pretended to be dead, the lazy
hamster might do the same to us. Then
we'd just have to break out of the hamster's
bin and return to our own one.

I explained my plan to Harry, and he agreed to give it a try.

When the lazy hamster stirred the next morning, we threw ourselves down on our sawdust and pretended to be dead.

I waited to hear the hamster cry with shock, but he just plodded over to his door and left.

This was going to be much tougher than I thought. The hamster wasn't just lazy. He was forgetful, too.

He hadn't even remembered we were there!

We tried again when the hamster came home, we tried again the following morning, and again the following evening.

This time he noticed us.

He spotted us, gasped, flung the lid off our cage and prodded us. We both managed to remain perfectly still. I heard him pacing around the room and squeaking with panic.

Then he picked us up and stomped out. I really hoped he was going to throw us in the bin, rather than bury us in the garden ...

We were about to find out ...

CHAPTER SEVEN

It turned out to be worse than I could have imagined. The lazy hamster didn't even bother taking us to the bin. Instead, he threw us in the TOILET!

We bobbed around in the bowl for a moment, then I heard the flush.

I held my breath as water gushed all around me. We swirled round and round, before getting sucked around a sharp bend and down a long pipe.

We tumbled into a pool of stinky sludge, while toilet water showered around us.

I stood up and wiped my face. The pipe was pitch black, so I couldn't see a thing.

OVER HERE.
ARE YOU OKAY?
JUST GIVE ME A MINUTE. I NEED TO FIND THE LIGHT ON MY SPACE COMMUNICATOR.

We were in a long sewer. The bottom was lined with a river of hamster poo so deep it came up to our knees. The sides were made from crumbly concrete with chunks missing.

We can still escape. If we follow the flow of the poo, we should end up in the sea. From there, we can swim back to land and find the spacebin.

I noticed wide circular holes above us.

I was about to say that they're the places the toilets flush into. But it looks like you've just found that out for yourself.

We trudged on for ages. At one point, I thought I could hear something scampering nearby, but when I turned there was nothing there.

Eventually, I could smell salty water as well as hamster poo. There was the distant sound of crashing waves.

We were getting close to the sea. We were almost free.

I raced ahead, desperate to be out of the poo river, but I slammed into something solid.

Harry caught up with me and shone his light on to it.

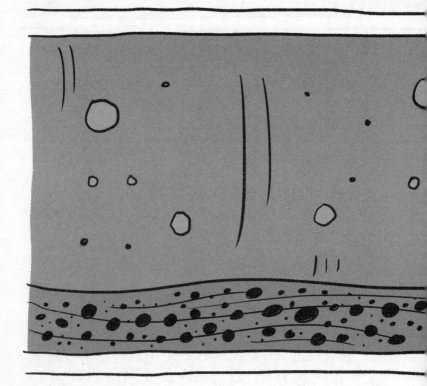

We'll never escape through the metal bars. We'll be trapped in this hamster poo forever. I'll never see Mum or Dad or Nuclear Dragon Slayer Henderson again.

Calm down. I think there might be another way out. Did you notice all those missing chunks in the walls? I think they might have been clawed by something. Let's find some and investigate.

Clawed? You want us to enter the lair of a creature with claws?

At least that means it's not a snake. Unless snakes have claws on this planet.

Just so you know, you're really not helping right now.

Images of horrible clawed monsters filled my mind as we looked for one of the holes. My knees felt weak, but I forced myself on. There was no other way to go.

We found one of the gaps in the concrete and Harry shone his light into it. There was a narrow passage beyond the missing chunks. Something must have accidentally burrowed into the sewer before smelling the hamster poo and turning back.

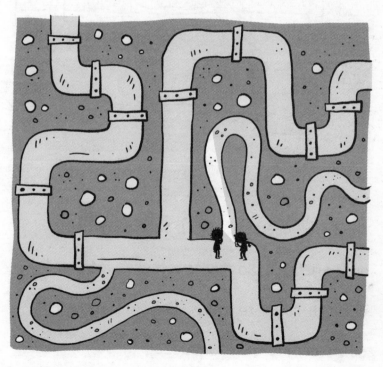

Harry climbed in, and I followed. The
passage was so narrow there was hardly
enough room to crawl. Dry soil showered
down on me as I squeezed through.

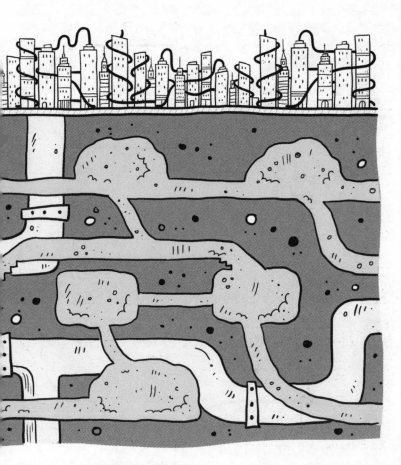

To my relief, the passage opened into a
much wider space. I got back to my feet
and wiped the dirt from my arms.

Shhh! Listen.

Something was pattering around ahead of us. It was making a fast murmuring noise.

Whatever it is, it sounds angry.

I'll use my space communicator to translate whatever it's saying. Most alien creatures can be reasoned with. And the ones that can't rarely ever have sharp fangs. And the ones that do hardly ever have fangs filled with venom.

Just to let you know, you're still not helping.

We followed the tunnel around a bend and Harry shone his light on to ...

...DOLDRUMS

CHAPTER EIGHT

I couldn't believe the teacher had mistaken us for THESE things. Now I'd met one, I was even more offended.

They had droopy mouths, pale skin and thin hair that was matted down to their heads. They were covered in slime and wearing dirty scraps of animal skin.

They didn't look like any humans I'd ever seen.

I suppose my little brother, David, gets quite slimy when he has a really bad cold. But even he's not THAT disgusting.

DAVID

Harry read something out from his space communicator. It sounded like furious muttering to me, but the doldrums seemed to understand. They nodded and led us up a passage lit by flickering torches.

That was easy. I told them we'd wandered into their warren by mistake and they agreed to take us back to the surface. It just goes to show how nice most aliens are if you're polite.

Hmm ... They don't seem very nice to me.

Every now and then, we'd pass a damp space where more of the miserable creatures were slumped in the mud and chewing worms.

Harry smiled and waved, but they just frowned.

The passage came out in a large hall that had been hollowed from the soil.

There was another tunnel sloping up ahead of us, but instead of leading us to it, the doldrums twisted our hands behind our backs and forced us sharply to the side.

Where are they taking us?

There were two wooden poles sticking out of the soil ahead of us. Small branches had been piled around the bottom of each one, and doldrums with flaming torches were standing beside them.

The doldrums shoved our backs against
the poles and tied us up.

I thought you said they were going to lead us to the surface?

It looks like my space communicator was wrong. What the doldrums were actually saying was, "We've caught you trespassing and we're going to burn you." If we get out of this alive, I'll write a very strong complaint letter to the company that made the translation app.

CHAPTER NINE

I managed to work the ropes loose while the doldrums were preparing the fire, but I still needed to work out how to get away.

I've got it! Remember the hamster teacher's lesson? He said the only way to calm doldrums was to burp on them. All we've got to do is belch on these creatures and we can escape.

But I can't burp! I've never been able to. I can fart, sneeze, vomit, hiccup and all the rest, but I never got the hang of burping.

Okay. Leave it to me.

I opened my mouth, drew in some air and turned to the doldrum next to me. It was all down to me now. I had to burp us to freedom.

The doldrums tried to grab us, but I burped every single one of them out of the way.

I worked the ropes loose and we ran into the tunnel at the end of the hall and kept going until we could see daylight.

The exit came into view.

There was a single doldrum standing in it. He was taller and stronger than the others, and must have been a guard.

He span round as we approached. I opened my mouth and swallowed air.

I tried to belch, but nothing came out.

I was out of burps.

CHAPTER TEN

The guard stomped towards us. I could hear the other doldrums scampering up the tunnel behind us. They'd already recovered.

What are you waiting for? Burp him away and we'll be free.

I haven't got any burps left. I've used them all up.

You've got to try. We only need one more.

I closed my eyes and imagined I was glugging an extra-large bottle of fizzy drink. I thought about all the gassy liquid washing down my throat and sloshing around in my stomach.

When I'd drained the pretend bottle, I opened my eyes. The guard was almost upon us. I opened my mouth ...

I'd tried so hard to burp, I'd made myself sick. It must've been all of those worm rations that Harry kept giving me.

It worked almost as well as a burp, though. The guard looked down at himself in confusion and we slipped past.

We kept walking and ended up in a flat field
at the side of a road. The sunlight was so
bright, I could hardly see.

But there was no time to let my eyes
adjust. The guard was coming after us,
and the other doldrums were streaming
out behind him.

We fled through tall, thick blades of grass
until we reached the side of the road.
I could see the hamster city in the distance,
with the Great Wheel rising high above it.

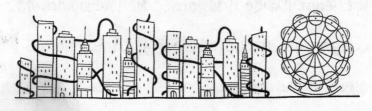

There was an empty plastic ball at the side of the road. We ran over to it and opened the hatch.

We leapt inside and locked it. The doldrums caught up with us and banged their hands against the plastic.

Harry got down on his hands and knees.

Come on! Let's get this thing moving!

I got down next to him and we tried to push.

NOTHING HAPPENED!

We're not heavy enough to get it going.

I tried throwing myself at the front of the ball, but it still didn't move.

Hundreds of doldrums were gathering outside the ball. I wondered if I should open the hatch and burp, but there were too many of them.

Even if I had a real bottle of fizzy pop, I wouldn't be able conjure up enough burps to defeat them all.

I've got an idea.

Harry turned to the doldrums. He did impressions of them, mimicking their slouching shoulders, droopy frowns and muttering voices. Then he pointed at them and laughed.

The doldrums pressed up against the plastic
and banged their fists harder and harder.
Their murmuring turned into fierce shrieking.

The ball rolled forwards on to the road.

What now? We'll have to make them really angry if they're going to push us all the way back to the city.

Now we're in the middle of the road. we just need to wait for another ball to come along and ...

A speeding hamster ball smacked into ours and sent us flying ahead.

The road sloped down and we picked up speed. We went faster and faster. I could hear angry squeaks from other hamsters as they steered out of the way.

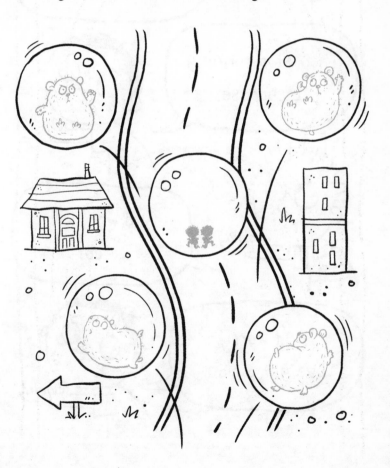

So err ... what do hamsters do when they want these things to slow down?

They stop running, I suppose.

And what will we do?

Don't worry. I've got a plan.

I could see the tall buildings of the city spinning towards us. If we didn't slow down soon, we'd crash right into one.

Harry was staring at his space communicator.

Stop looking at that! We need to find a way to stop this ball before it smashes into something!

Hang on. The spacebin is just about to come back into range. Wait for it ... Got it!

The spacebin appeared inside the ball with us. We leapt in and pulled the lid shut.

Harry reached for the controls, but the bin began to clatter around so quickly it was impossible to get to them. We both reached out desperately as the bin tumbled inside the spinning ball.

Finally, Harry managed to pull the lever
to get us off the planet.

CHAPTER ELEVEN

Harry made the spacebin return to the time just after we'd left, exactly like he said he would. If anyone had been watching, they'd only have seen a bin disappear and reappear. But to us it had been a draining couple of days of wading through poo, running away from weird creatures and spinning in massive wheels.

I clambered out, said goodbye to Harry and
staggered back home.

Mum spotted me coming in through the
back door. I tried to say hello to her,
but I was so tired the noise just came
out as a grunt.

What have you
been doing? Those
clothes were fresh
on this morning.

I hadn't even thought about what a state
I was in. No wonder Mum was shocked.

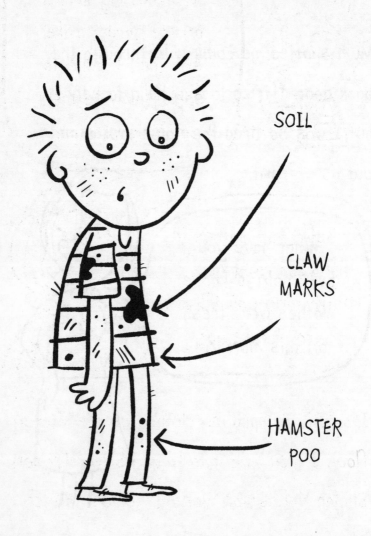

SOIL

CLAW
MARKS

HAMSTER
POO

Err ... I accidentally scratched my jumper on the garden rake. And then I fell into some soil. And then some hamster poo.

Get those clothes in the wash right now. I'm not having you stinking the house out.

I quickly dumped my clothes on the kitchen floor. I didn't want to leave Nuclear Dragon Slayer Henderson alone a moment longer.

I raced upstairs to my room. I was right.

I'd left the hamster's cage open. But ...

HE WAS SAFE!

He hadn't escaped, or been kidnapped, or been flushed down the toilet or anything else. He was just sitting in his cage as usual, staring at me and twitching his little pink nose.

Thanks for being boring, Nuclear Dragon Slayer Henderson. Now I know what it's like to be you. I'll never be rude again.

Grab your copy of Cosmic Colin's
next adventure!

Out now!